egg

kevin henkes

 greenwillow books

egg

Egg

Copyright © 2017 by Kevin Henkes

All rights reserved. Printed in the United States of America.
For information address HarperCollins Children's Books,
a division of HarperCollins Publishers,
195 Broadway, New York, NY 10007.
www.harpercollinschildrens.com

Brown ink and watercolor paint
were used to prepare the full-color art.
The text type is Futura BT Light.

Library of Congress Cataloging-in-Publication Data

Names: Henkes, Kevin, author, illustrator.
Title: Egg / Kevin Henkes.
Description: First edition. | New York, NY : Greenwillow Books, [2017] |
Summary: Three little birds crack their way out of eggs and fly away,
leaving one egg sitting all alone until the three chicks come back
and discover a friendly baby alligator has finally hatched.
Identifiers: LCCN 2016005267 | ISBN 9780062408723 (trade ed.) |
ISBN 9780062408730 (lib. bdg.)
Subjects: | CYAC: Eggs—Fiction. | Birth—Fiction. |
Animals—Infancy—Fiction. | Friendship—Fiction. |
BISAC: JUVENILE FICTION / Concepts / General. | JUVENILE FICTION /
Nature & the Natural World / General (see also headings under Animals).
Classification: LCC PZ7.H389 Eg 2017 | DDC [E] —dc23
LC record available at https://lccn.loc.gov/2016005267

16 17 18 19 20 WOR 10 9 8 7 6 5 4 3 2 1
First Edition

Greenwillow Books

for s. k.

egg

egg

egg

egg

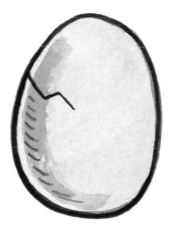

crack

crack

crack

egg

surprise!

surprise!

surprise!

egg

good-bye

good-bye

good-bye

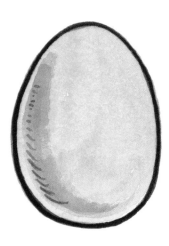

egg

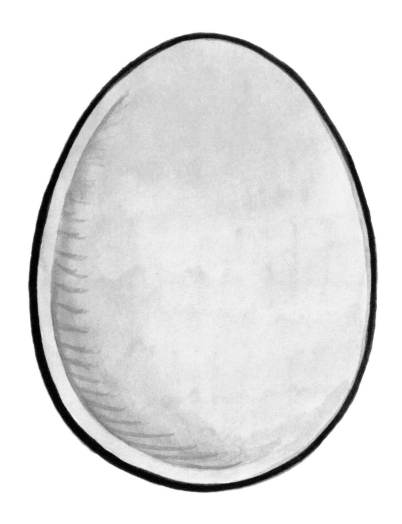

waiting

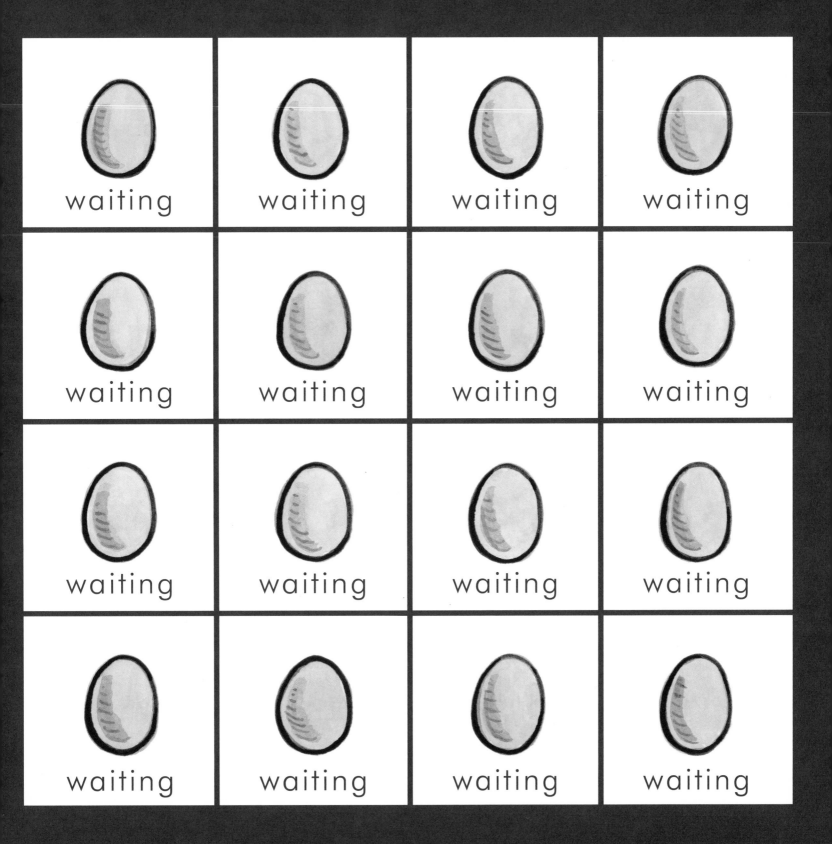

listen

peck-peck-peck

peck-peck-peck

peck-peck-peck

peck-peck-peck

peck-peck-peck

peck-peck-peck peck-peck-peck peck-peck-peck peck-peck-peck

peck-peck-peck peck-peck-peck peck-peck-peck peck-peck-peck

peck-peck-peck peck-peck-peck peck-peck-peck peck-peck-peck

peck-peck-peck peck-peck-peck peck-peck-peck peck-peck-peck

crack

surprise!

alone

sad

lonely

miserable

friends

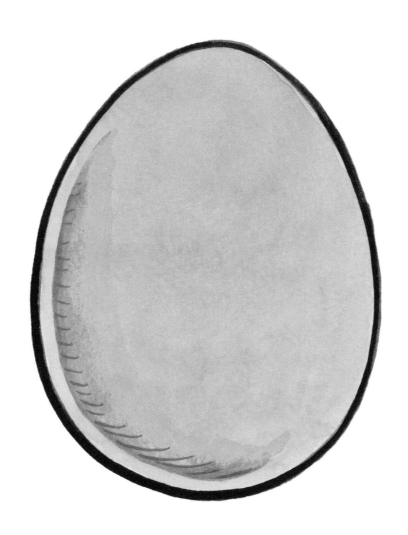

the end . . .

maybe